CHILDHOOD

CHILDHOOD

GREG SCHAFFER

SECOND CHANCE PUBLISHING
FRANKLIN, TENNESSEE

Second Chance Publishing – PO Box 680551 – Franklin, Tennessee 37068-0551

https://www.secondchancebook.org

ISBN: 978-1-7330668-1-5 (paperback)
ISBN: 978-1-7330668-2-2 (ebook)

Ten-year-old Katie Whetley crossed her arms and stared out the Nortonville Elementary School classroom window. She scowled at Joey Barbetti swinging freely on the playground's monkey bars during lunch recess. She hated the name Joseph, but he refused to let her call him Joey, or Joe, or Jay. Or boyfriend.

She returned to her desk in a huff. She saw no reason to go out for recess today. He never talked to her. Instead, she buried her head in a Nancy Drew mystery and hoped tales of teenage sleuthing would make her forget him. She liked that word, *sleuthing*. It sounded like something water did in a tub when you moved your arms around.

Out of the corner of her eye, she caught Mrs. Perry

at the door. She hunched closer to the old, musty pages, hoping the teacher hadn't seen her.

"Caitlyn, why aren't you enjoying the beautiful sunny day?"

She put down the book. "It's Katie. I wanna read."

"Katie, I encourage reading, but you need to get outside sometimes too."

She's doing it again.

"I get enough exercise working on the farm. I want to read."

Mrs. Perry's flowery, summer dress flowed when she strolled over to Katie's desk. If it made a sound, it would be *sleuth, sleuth.*

"It's not just the exercise. All of your friends are out there."

"Hmph. Not all of them are my friends."

"What's the matter?"

What was she, like thirty? She wouldn't understand.

"Do you like a boy?"

Katie froze.

"I know what it's like to like a boy." Mrs. Perry slid into the chair beside Katie.

Katie's mouth dropped. "You do?"

"Sure. When I was in fourth grade, about your age, I was totally in love with a fifth grader. He never knew I existed then."

Her stomach sank. "What happened to him?"

"I married him."

"Really?" Katie closed the Nancy Drew book.

Mrs. Perry nodded, her shoulder-length brown hair swaying with each bob. "It took a while. We lost touch for several years, but we reconnected, and right after college he asked me to marry him."

College?

Katie slumped.

"What's wrong?"

"That's a long time."

Mrs. Perry laughed. Katie didn't get the joke.

"It's not as long as you think." She stood. "Okay, you can stay here for the last ten minutes of recess. I'll let you get back to your reading."

After Mrs. Perry exited the room, Katie stared out the window at Joey hanging upside down, laughing. She often saw him playing in his back yard while she helped her father with the barn chores. It seemed that was all he ever did. She wished he liked to read. She let her stare linger for a moment, then opened the pages and returned to the mysterious world of Nancy Drew.

#

The school bus's rear tires hit a pothole on the

gravel road and the rear lurched upward, prompting Katie to scream with glee in unison with the other children. Another momentary rise out of her seat caused her Memorial Day school project to shift, and she came down on the edge of the box. She lifted the diorama and inspected it, a bit saddened at the damage after all the time she and her father had spent creating it. Her younger brother Evan had helped, gluing the green plastic soldiers to the base. Her project had earned three gold stars, the best in the class.

The bus slowed to a stop. Joey was always the first one out. He sprinted to the front door of the yellow house. He said he liked some afternoon TV show called *Clone Wars*. Though she didn't care for anything related to *Star Wars*, she'd enjoyed that momentary spark of attention he'd given her. The bus pulled away as Joey disappeared behind the aluminum screen door. The tear in the screen flapped up and down.

She checked the zipper of her backpack as the bus slowed. She waited until the bus came to a complete stop before she stood. She didn't want another lecture from Pat, the bus driver. She didn't like Pat. Pat never smiled, and she smelled like cigarettes and was always yelling at somebody or something. She said the F-word once.

Katie stepped over the painted rocks that lined the front of the lawn just before the grass ended and the paved road began. Pat never stopped the bus in front of their gravel driveway as Dad had directed many times. Each time he asked, Pat stopped a little farther away.

Katie paused to savor the sweetness of the fresh-cut grass then bounded to her house's side door. Uncle Henry always called their home "the White House." Once she'd asked him why. With a laugh, he'd responded, "Because it's white."

"Dad?" No response.

She dumped her book bag and the damaged diorama on the floor. One of the tiny green soldiers separated from its glue base and clicked onto the hardwood floor next to her bag. "Figures." She grabbed the Nancy Drew mystery from her bag and plopped in Dad's big chair in the living room.

Movement outside the large picture window that faced the barn and cornfield in the distance distracted her from the mystery. She tracked her father as he walked from the garage to the barn. He was behind schedule cleaning the stalls. Dinner would be late. She closed the book and headed for the barn.

Hunter Whetley raked hay in the nearest stall, the first of four to clean before feeding the horses and turning them out. When he saw Katie, he leaned against the tip of the rake, his white work gloves showing drip paths from sweat.

"I'll get the muck bucket." Katie grabbed her worn pair of leather gloves from the shelf near the tractor and positioned the bucket so her father could scoop the manure into it more easily.

"I'll get a new tire for the wheelbarrow tomorrow."

She scrunched her nose after he dumped a load in. "Dad, did you marry Mom after college?"

He stopped mid-toss. "College? Why do you ask?"

"Mrs. Perry married her husband right after college."

"Oh. No, it was during college." He resumed his motion, a couple of manure chips missing the bucket from the loss of momentum.

"How long after was I born?"

"About a year later."

She glanced at the silver horseshoe, ends up for luck, that Dad had nailed above the barn entrance when he and Mom bought the place after they'd married. "And then Evan two years after me, when …"

Her father donned the same faraway expression he always did whenever she mentioned Evan's birth. She should have known better. She regretted bringing it up.

"She was a strong woman, just not strong enough." He scooped the deflected remnants and wiped his forehead with one of the red bandannas Mom had given him when they'd bought the farm. "We're done here. Next stall."

She decided she didn't want to talk about Evan, or Mom, either. Her stomach growled, but the chores needed to get done first. As always.

Her father opened the next stall. "Why do you want to know when we got married?"

She kept her head low. She didn't want to divulge her secret about Joey. "I dunno."

The chickens in the coop at the edge of the back yard clucked. "You'd better get the eggs," Dad said. "And take Evan with you."

"Do I have to?" The protest wasn't about the eggs.

His stern eyes provided the answer. She rambled out the barn side door, slamming it.

"Watch the door," he shouted after her.

She walked across the yard to find Evan drifting in his swing and staring at the sky. The chickens clucked louder than usual. She searched the sky. No clouds.

Dad always says chickens talking means there's bad weather coming.

She wondered what about the sky fascinated Evan so much. *Maybe he knows it's going to rain.* Locked in a world with almost no vocabulary and a penchant for spontaneous wandering, her younger brother seemed happy most of the time in his private existence. She both pitied and envied that. It wasn't his fault he wasn't like all the rest.

"C'mon Evan. Time to get eggs." He followed without resistance, until a butterfly crossed their path. He tore across the yard toward the cornfield, chasing the flapping colors.

"Evan, come back here. Dad's not going to be happy." She sprinted after him.

She caught up with him at the edge of the cornfield. Evan stared into the tall stalks. The butterfly was gone.

She wagged her index finger at him. "You have got to listen. Dad's behind again, and if we're going to eat before bedtime you have to behave."

He smiled wordlessly.

The butterfly returned.

He began a sprint toward the front yard.

Not the road. That's even worse.

Katie pumped her arms but could not keep up with Evan. She turned the corner and saw him lying at the driveway edge, crying.

She pointed at the bleeding scraped knee. "See what you've done now? We're both gonna get it from Dad."

A tire skidded on the gravel. Joey Barbetti stood over his banana seat bicycle.

For a moment, everything froze.

"What are you looking at, Joey?"

"It's Joseph." He flipped the bike to the direction of his house down the road and pedaled away.

She scowled at him. Why did Joey choose this moment to ride by?

Evan sniffed and pointed to the chicken coop.

She led him by the hand. "You're right, little brother. Let's get the eggs."

2

Sixth Grade (Fall 2007)

"Now gently crack the egg and let the yolk drop into the measuring cup."

Katie did exactly as Mrs. Noonan, the home economics teacher, instructed. She had been making eggs for Dad and Evan for years.

"Nice job, Katie," Mrs. Noonan said.

Katie grabbed another egg. "We have a chicken coop on our farm."

"Oh? What kind of chickens do you raise?"

Katie paused. "I dunno. Regular farm chickens, I guess."

Katie turned at the cackling behind her. Egg yolk ran through Joey's and Dennis's fingers. Each tried to slap the other. Slimy egg flew everywhere. A blob landed on Katie's face.

"Stop. You'll mess up my book." She scowled at the boys, then wiped egg white from her cheek and off the cover of *To Kill a Mockingbird*.

Mrs. Noonan stepped between the two boys to break up the sloppy slap fest, then grabbed a paper towel from Katie's table and blotted her blouse.

Joey caught Katie's eye and smirked. Her heart quickened from his glance.

"Whatcha starin' at, dufus?" he said.

She looked away quickly and wiped another drop of egg off the cover of the paperback. Scout wouldn't take his teasing.

"Don't let them get to you." Her new friend Lynn prepped the skillet with cooking spray.

Katie cracked the second egg into the glass measuring cup. "I saw you running past my house this morning. Why do you run?"

Lynn shrugged. "I dunno. I like it, I guess. And I'm good at it." She smirked. "And I get to run with the boys."

"Like who?"

"Steve Sully, Greg Lopez, Joey Barbetti..."

Joey?

Katie swallowed, then added a hint of water to the eggs and whisked the mixture. "You're on the cross-country team, right?"

"Yeah, I was excited to join. That's my favorite thing about getting to junior high."

"What do you do?"

Lynn placed the skillet onto the stove with a clank. "We run. Duh."

Katie's face flushed. "How far?"

"The races are three miles."

Katie almost dropped the glass measuring cup holding the eggs. "Three miles?"

"It sounds like a lot, but it isn't. Some days at practice we run five."

Dad would never let me miss afternoon chores to run.

Katie poured the thoroughly beaten egg mixture into the frying pan. "I could never run five miles."

"Sure you could." Lynn used the rubber spatula to stir the eggs like the short-order cooks at the Waffle House near the interstate. "I couldn't make an omelet two weeks ago. My grandmother taught me."

"I thought you said your grandmother died."

"My other grandmother. Check out this creation."

"But I helped."

"Right. And I'll help you run. I'll draw up a schedule. I started with four laps. That's a mile." Lynn pointed with the spatula out the window to the track behind the school.

"A mile? That's impossible. I'd need too many stops to breathe."

"Give me the cheese." Lynn sprinkled the shredded cheddar and flipped the eggs. "Look at this beauty. Two weeks. Nothing is impossible."

Katie glanced behind her at Joey, immersed in cooking eggs, and let go a slight smile.

Nothing is impossible.

#

The new preacher of St. Paul's Methodist Church, hair parted on two sides and spiked in the middle like a greasy pyramid, met Katie, Evan, and their father at the door. "Thank you for coming."

Preachers always say that.

"Thank you, Reverend Andrews. That was a wonderful sermon." Her father shook the God-man's hand.

"Well, thank you, Hunter. It is Hunter, right?"

Her father smiled. Hunter was his middle name. His first name was Boris. He never told anyone that. "Yes, Reverend."

Katie turned, still fixated on the preacher's odd coiffure, and bumped into Joey outside the church entrance.

"Hey, Katie."

She expected a different greeting. Maybe church softened him.

"Hey." She hoped he might stop and talk to her, but then she noticed a hint of drool on Evan's chin. Joey did not wait around during her search for a napkin in her small purse. She wiped the spit before it dripped off.

Opportunity lost.

Evan pointed up with a wild laugh. She raised her eyes to the sky.

"I don't see it, little brother." She wondered what he spied in the clear, blue sky that she could not. A plane?

They had to ride in her father's work vehicle because the truck was at McCauley's for new tires. She didn't like the smell of cigarettes in the cab. Her father didn't smoke, but his coworker did.

Her father drove the van out of the church's parking lot and turned in an opposite direction from their house.

"Where are we going?" Katie asked.

"I thought I'd treat you guys to Dairy Queen."

Evan squealed in delight.

"No."

Her father stopped at the town's only traffic light and turned to her. "Why not?"

The thought of running after ice cream nauseated her. "I just don't want to."

"Evan wants ice cream. You don't have to eat."

Evan flailed his arms around. He loved ice cream. Dad was right. It wasn't all about her.

She smiled at him and tousled his hair. "Okay."

#

Katie laced up her running shoes. She'd only ever used them for walking and school, never for anything athletic, except gym class.

What am I doing?

The knot in her stomach tightened harder than the laces. She hated the pink shorts Dad got her for Christmas, but she had nothing else to wear for this experiment.

She stood and arched her back, then clumsily stretched her right leg, then left, to emulate what she had seen Lynn do. Her balance wavered while she held her ankle behind her back with her hand. Only the handle of the screen door saved her from an inadvertent fall.

Evan cackled from inside the screen door.

She pointed at him. "Don't try to talk me out of this."

This she could do, would do; something for her,

and not just for school, or the farm, or her father. Or Evan.

She declared herself warmed up for the run and walked the gravel driveway to the edge of the road, turned to the right, and placed her hands on her hips. The large tree at the corner of Cleveland and Finny roads a half-mile away——her target——tempted and encouraged her.

So far.

She walked: right foot, left foot, right foot. After ten steps she broke into a slow jog, the first time ever, outside of gym class or recess——on the odd occasion when she chose to play outside rather than read. Awkward plants of her feet propelled her forward at a pace slightly above walking. She grinned.

Running. I'm running.

Within a minute, her breathing increased and her heart beat faster. She would have to overcome the new sensation of near breathlessness if she were to make the goal from Lynn's schedule, Finny and back. A whole mile.

And this is just the first day. This is crazy.

Her heavy breathing did not drown out the pop of the knobby tires against the gravel behind her. She winced at the idea of a stranger witnessing her first attempts at running, but she didn't stop.

It wasn't a stranger. It was Joey.

He pulled up beside her on his bicycle. "Hey, I didn't know you run."

She concentrated on her feet, ignoring both him and the cramp developing in her midsection. Maybe he would just pass her. She wished she hadn't worn the pink shorts he, and others, teased her about.

Joey slowed his pedaling to keep pace with her, though she could tell by the way the bike wobbled he was finding it difficult on the gravel road. "How long have you been running?"

"I started this week." Today. Two minutes ago. And talking while running——it was not easy.

"I think that's really cool."

She stopped, not because of the cramp but out of surprise. She bent over to try to catch her breath and hide her reaction. "What?"

"That's cool. You know, I run, too."

Yeah. Cross-country. With Lynn.

She stood, her chest heaving for air. "I didn't know. You like it?"

He flipped his straight black hair away from of his eyes. "I dunno. It's okay. Keeps me in shape for baseball."

"I'm going to Finny and back," she said with a purposeful hint of pride and resumed her run.

He pedaled slowly beside her. "That's what, a mile?"

She nodded.

"Have fun." With that he turned the bike. The pop of the gravel against the tires faded but she didn't look back.

He said my running was cool.

She reached the large oak tree at the corner of Cleveland and Finny and turned. Her house seemed so far away, but her old self was farther.

3

Ninth Grade (Fall 2010)

Katie strolled down the hallway past the row of orange metal lockers with confidence, her spirit buoyed by making the JV cross-country team.

"Katie."

She stopped at Felipe's locker. The new boy from California had piercing blue eyes and long, unruly dark hair.

"You're a runner, right? Do you run in the morning, before sunrise?"

"Sometimes."

"Why?"

"Because it's cooler then."

He grinned. "No, it's because you want to finish before you wake up and realize what you're doing." He poked her side. "C'mon, you know it's true."

She laughed. "It's not."

"Seriously, congratulations on making the cross-country team."

"How'd you know?"

He pointed at the letter patch in the mesh pocket of her backpack. "Cool stuff. I gotta run myself, gonna be late for math."

Katie let her stare linger at Felipe walking away, then strolled down the hallway in the opposite direction.

"Hey, how's it going?" Joey matched her walking pace.

"Okay." She flipped her brown hair away from her eyes. She liked that his last class was next to hers.

"Where are the girls running this afternoon?"

"I think the middle school four-mile circle, why?"

"I dunno, just asking."

She stopped at her locker as Lynn arrived at the one beside hers. Lynn flashed a wide smile and showed off her newly straightened, braces-free teeth.

Always showing up at exactly the same time.

Joey locked his eyes on Lynn. "Where are you guys running for practice today?"

I just told you.

"Don't know, Coach hasn't told us." Lynn twirled a few strands of her red hair with her finger and lowered her head, eyes fixated on Joey. "I think we're going past the middle school."

Flirt.

"I like that route."

Hello, there's someone else here too.

Katie stayed silent as she retrieved *Great Expectations* from her backpack, then placed the bag in the locker.

Joey leaned his lanky frame in closer and propped his hand above Lynn's locker, the t-shirt sleeve pulled up enough to provide Katie with a whiff of afternoon perspiration. She repressed a gag.

Lynn kept her coy expression on Joey. She pointed to the rear of the cubbyhole at the top of the locker. "Hey, can you grab that book in the back for me? It's just out of my reach."

Joey leaned closer to Lynn, the obvious intended effect. "Sure."

Oh, please.

Katie shut her metal locker door with a bit more force than necessary and secured the lock. A five-hundred-page novel was more interesting than this dribble.

#

"Now pay attention and don't get distracted. Don't take out the fence line again."

Katie grimaced at her father, who winked back at her before he returned to applying grease to the tractor's ball bearings. Evan stood by, rag in hand. Assisting Dad helped Evan more than it did him.

She had snagged the new fence on the east side last month with the bush hog and ripped open a three-foot hole, that was true, but not due to distraction. It wouldn't have happened if her father had secured the wire to the brace post. They both understood that.

She climbed into the idling Kubota's seat and drove toward the east side grazing field. Since the horses grazed in the other field while this one recovered, the gate was open. No need to secure it if there was no chance of livestock escaping.

The hum of the engine soothed her as it always had since her toddler days when her father would hold her with his left arm and steer with his right. He had taught her every outside chore on the farm except the landscape maintenance around the house. She enjoyed the solitude of bush hogging.

Her phone buzzing in her coverall front pocket prompted her to shut down the tractor's engine despite her father's mandate. She smiled at the number.

"How'd you do on the social studies test?" Felipe asked.

She glanced toward the barn. "I can't talk now." She placed the phone back in her pocket. Her father may not have peered around the edge of the run-in shed to shoot her a reminder to continue, but he could still hear. He knew she had stopped the tractor. Besides, revisiting the test was the last thing she wanted to do. She restarted the Kubota and resumed the bush hogging.

She hadn't cut more than a few feet when the phone buzzed again. She resisted the urge to answer as she navigated the first turn past the patched fence, careful not to get close to the brace post. A busted fence or a bad cut was worse than no cut at all. The last time she rushed, her father had commandeered her phone for three days.

She turned back toward the house to see Evan walk from the yard into the cornfield.

Not again.

She shut down the tractor and ran toward the field.

"Evan?"

Silence.

She navigated the rows, careful not to damage the stalks and caught a small rustle off to her right.

"Evan, come here."

She moved slowly. When Evan got lost in the cornfield last week, it took her and Dad nearly a half-hour to find him.

A flash of his blue jacket to her right caught her eye. She rushed, cracking a stalk in the process, and grabbed Evan's hand.

"You have got to stop doing this."

Evan stopped and looked at her, then began crying.

She wrapped her arms around him. "It's okay, little brother." She ignored the phone buzzing.

#

The nerves ate at Katie's gut as she sat down. Today they'd get the test back. Her grade point average couldn't handle a bad mark.

Felipe paused at her desk two rows in front of his. "Hey, what's the smartest state?"

He knows I'm terrible at geography.

She mustered up a smile. "I dunno."

"Alabama."

"Alabama?"

"Yeah, it has four A's and one B." He chuckled as he walked to his desk while Mrs. Thomas passed out the graded exams.

Katie glanced at the test paper, then slapped it on the desk.

A C+. That's great.

She closed her eyes, then opened them to review the test. She had misidentified several of the Eastern Europe countries on the map.

She felt a tap on her shoulder.

"Psst," Lynn said. "How'd you do?"

She held up the paper for Lynn to see the red C+ on top.

"Oh. Sorry."

"I'm a little disappointed with the test grades," Mrs. Thomas said. "The average was a C."

At least I beat the average.

Katie surveyed the room. Not many happy faces from her vantage point. She figured those in the front earned grades they were satisfied with. She caught the back of Joey's head, always in the front row, and wondered what he got.

Katie raised her hand.

"Yes, Katie?"

"Mrs. Thomas, I think the test was a little unfair."

"Why is that?"

"Why do we need to know where these countries are? We can just use the internet for that."

Mrs. Thomas smiled. "Believe it or not, the internet hasn't been around forever."

"But we have it now." She lowered her hand, suddenly not so sure of her defense tactic.

"Sure. And before that we had maps in huge books called atlases. Before that, parchment scrolls. Before that, cave paintings," Felipe said.

She turned at Felipe chuckling two rows behind her. She let her stare linger until she realized what she was doing, then snapped her head to face the front of the class. The warmth in her face remained.

Lynn tapped her shoulder again. "Hey. Joey and I are going to the rink this evening. You want to come?"

"I can't."

"Your Dad can let you out of one night of chores, can't he?"

She avoided the awkwardness of activities with them. "Nope."

She felt Lynn's breath against her ear. "Besides, I hear Felipe's going to be there."

Katie's heart raced but she did not move. "Really?"

"Yeah. Don't worry, I don't think he noticed you staring at him."

Katie glanced over at Mrs. Thomas writing on the white board with her back to the class. "I did not."

"Oh, come on, your eyes bugged out."

Katie felt the redness in her cheeks return. "He is kind of cute, isn't he?"

"Kind of? He's a stud," Lynn whispered.

"I guess."

"I heard Sue is after him. They were at the Dairy Queen yesterday after school."

"Something you ladies want to share with the class?"

Katie shook her head. Mrs. Thomas stood still for a moment, then continued the lesson. She wondered if Felipe wanted to get away from Nortonville as badly as she did. Not that it mattered if she didn't keep her grades up. Running scholarships required good times *and* grades.

4

The footsteps from her greatest competitor and best friend pounded behind Katie as she rounded the last turn on the track. This time she was determined to beat Lynn. This time, she would win——the last meet of their junior year.

Her lungs screamed for air and her legs protested with pain as she sprinted the final straightaway of the girls 3200-meter run at the Collierville Invitational Track Meet. To hear each breath meant Lynn had to be almost beside her, about to pass her.

No. Not this time.

Katie stretched out her arms and flung her chest forward as she crossed the finish line with Lynn less than a second behind her. The formidable one-two long-distance punch of the Nortonville High girls' track team had just flipped positions.

They bent over and leaned hands on thighs to catch their breath. Katie smiled at Lynn, a silent acknowledgment of the momentous occasion, then vomited in the grass.

Lynn put her arm around Katie's midsection. "Are you okay?"

Katie nodded while still bent over and wiped her chin with the back of her hand. She had given the race her all. This would not make for a flattering photo. She slowly rose and glanced at the other finishers. "I'll be fine."

"Did you see our times?"

Katie noticed the scoreboard and screamed. "Holy cow." She hugged Lynn and didn't care about the sweat that drenched them both, or any of the remaining slobber on her chin. She'd beaten her best friend and broken the school record.

"Congratulations, ladies." Joey handed them each a cold-water bottle.

Katie drank several gulps to quell the nausea. "Thanks. That was truly epic."

Lynn drank about a third of her bottle and then poured the rest over her head "Ahhhh. That feels so good." She put a hand on Joey's shoulder. "Thanks, sweetie."

Katie cringed internally but kept a neutral posture as usual when Lynn spoke cutesy to her boyfriend. She bent over to massage her sore calves as Felipe approached.

Good, I won't be the odd one anymore.

"Congrats. You flew." Felipe's broad smile accentuated his deep blue eyes.

She smiled and wiped her chin with a hand towel, just in case. "Thank you, kind sir."

Felipe offered another towel. "You should let your hair down so it can flutter in the breeze as you blast past everyone."

Is he flirting with me?

She blushed and covered part of her face with the towel, pretending to wipe more sweat. "It keeps me cooler when it's up. Though today it's so hot, nothing helps."

Felipe nodded. "Want to grab a Coke?"

"Sure."

Where's Sue?

"Don't mind us. You just go on," Joey said.

The sound of Joey's voice made her want to crawl under the bleachers. She had forgotten he and Lynn were behind her. "You guys want to come?"

Lynn shook her head. "I have to shower and get home. My aunt's coming in and we're going to Olive Garden."

"Woohoo, live it up," Felipe said.

Joey frowned at Felipe, then faced Katie. "You sure you're okay? You still look a little green."

Gee, thanks.

"I'm fine. A Coke will do me good."

"If you need anything, let me know." Joey put his arm around Lynn and they left her with Felipe.

"I wish I could run like that," Felipe said as they began the walk to the Mapco, the opposite direction of Joey's truck.

"It's my ticket out of here."

"Are you planning to go to the University of Memphis, like Joey and Lynn?"

"No, forty miles west is still too close."

"I guess I understand. It must be a pain to deal with that stuff at home."

She stopped before they reached the edge of the school property. "Excuse me?"

Felipe shuffled his feet. "I, uh—"

"No, please, I want to hear what you mean."

"It's just that your brother—"

You insensitive— "Let me draw you a picture. Evan is the most special guy I know. And you know what? That's all I have to say to you."

"But—"

"Bye, Felipe."

#

An hour later, Felipe's callous remark about Evan still steamed her. She stopped on the way to the barn to see Evan in the backyard swing, lazily drifting back and forth, staring up. She sat next to him and put an arm around his shoulders. "Do you think it will rain, little brother?"

Evan grunted with a grin and pointed at the clouds. He would welcome new drops with an eager, outstretched tongue.

She tousled his hair and frowned at the sky. Those towering clouds meant thunderstorms were likely coming soon. "Stay here, Superman. I'm going to try to mow before those drops fall from the sky."

At the barn, she planted her feet but not wide enough to keep her balance when she yanked the drive shaft up to the mower connection point. She lurched back and slipped, slammed her hand against the shaft, and shouted in pain.

"Can I help you with that?" Joey's calm, deep voice appeared out of nowhere.

Why are you here?

"Thanks." Katie shook her hand to dispel the pain as Joey connected the shaft to the tractor with minimal effort. She offered him one of her father's red rags.

He wiped his hands on his worn jeans instead. "Is something bothering you?"

"How can you tell?"

He produced a racquetball from his jeans pocket and began tossing it up and down. "C'mon. I know you. Felipe, right?"

She examined the back of her hand. A little red, no broken skin.

"He's a tool." Joey began bouncing the racquetball off the side of the barn.

"What makes you say that?"

He stopped tossing the ball. "I'm a guy. I know guys."

"Then why did you let me go with him?"

"Because you needed to see for yourself." He held the ball in front of her. "And you did. Are you all right?"

"I guess." She checked the tractor's oil level. "Why aren't you with Lynn at Olive Garden?"

He resumed tossing the ball. "They haven't gotten back from picking up her aunt at the airport. Plane delayed."

She secured the dipstick. "Her aunt's from Ireland, right? I've always wanted to see Stonehenge."

"That's in England." The ball sailed into a stall. He leaned back against a pole and chewed on a stalk of hay, seemingly unconcerned about the lost racquetball. The top three buttons of his plaid shirt were unfastened, revealing a wisp of black chest hair.

Stop it.

"I don't much care for traveling," he said as he adjusted the angle of his worn straw cowboy hat.

"How would you know? You're like me. Our extravagant vacations involve heading to Nashville."

"I went to New York once."

She shook her head. "School band trips don't count."

"Yeah, they do. That was a great time, marching in the parade. Those floats are huge. Wouldn't ever want to live there though." He took off his hat and swatted her backside. "You're just jealous."

Well, yeah.

"Of New York City? Come on." She glanced at the clouds. "Dad won't let me have the car tomorrow night if I don't get this done."

He put his hat back on and tilted his head upward. "You really think you're gonna cut an acre of grass before that gets here?" He pointed at a tall, gray cloud, close enough that she could make out the virga that had developed below it.

"It's still dry. It's evaporating."

He sauntered over to her. "You may be horrible

in geography, but you know your weather. You do know we're under a thunderstorm watch, right?"

"It's late May in West Tennessee. We're always under a thunderstorm watch." She enjoyed the breeze in her face, but he was right. That cell would arrive sooner than later.

He grabbed a tarp. "Come on, let's cover the tractor and fire up the TV to watch *Breaking Bad*."

She wiped her hands and tossed the red rag in a bucket. "Oh, see, there it is. You're just here because we get AMC."

"Well, yeah, we only get four channels on a good day." He flashed that crazy, crooked, sexy Harrison Ford smile.

Stop it.

#

Katie halted at Finny Lane, stopped her Garmin, and noted the time. Not bad for a run in the hot June mid-morning sun. She finished the last of her Gatorade from her belt bottle.

The familiar sound of brakes squeaking brought a smile to her face. She turned as Joey pulled up next to her in his old faded-red Chevy pickup.

"How far did you go?" Lynn asked from the front passenger seat.

"Eight."

"Oh, a light run I see," Joey said. "You want a ride back?"

She shook her head. "I like walking the last half mile as a cool down."

"I remember when you first started running, you could barely make it to Finny and back."

She nodded. "I would have made it the first time if someone hadn't interrupted me."

Joey pointed at the twisted Finny Road signpost in the distance, one of the remaining indicators of the windstorm that had hit the area in May. "Yeah, well, with your huffing and puffing, I thought I'd have to pick you up and carry you on my bike back to your house."

"I wasn't that bad."

He turned back at her. "Yeah, actually you were, but look at you now. Star athlete."

So long as I get that scholarship.

She clicked the empty bottle back in its belt holder. "I'd better get walking."

Joey rolled up his plaid shirt sleeves. "You sure you don't want a ride?"

She nodded. "I'm sure, but thanks."

"We're going to Dairy Queen," Lynn said. "Want us to bring you anything?"

She doesn't really mean that.

"Nah, but thanks."

Joey put the truck in gear and rolled through the dirt road intersection toward the small town center. Through the dusty back window she caught Lynn leaning in as Joey put his arm around her. She imagined she was the one leaning in against Joey's shoulder, then shook off the pangs of jealousy.

She turned toward the white house of her childhood a half-mile away. Her times and grades almost guaranteed the scholarship, and her escape.

College.

5

Twelfth Grade (Spring 2014)

Katie squeezed next to Joey to make room for Lynn on the front seat of Joey's truck. Lynn's powerful scent from that new bottle of perfume from Dillard's arrived before she did. Sandwiched between Lynn and Joey's cheap cologne he kept in his gym locker, Katie regretted accepting the ride.

"I've gotta stop at the Co-op and pick up a few shavings. Do your folks need anything?"

Katie sniffed. "No. Can you turn on the AC?"

Joey flashed his crooked smile. "Sure."

The flow of air eased Katie's irritation and arrested her urge to sneeze. "What'd you think about this case?"

The truck lurched as it struck a pothole and Joey banged his hand against the steering wheel. "Man, another of those and I'm going to lose a tire. I dunno. It's interesting, I guess."

"Which one are you nerds studying now?" Katie caught a hint of sarcasm in Lynn's voice.

"Roe versus Wade," Joey said.

Lynn whistled. "Oh. The biggie. Well, I'm set on that one."

Katie eyed Lynn sideways. "Really? What's your stand?"

"Wow, you need to ask?" Lynn shook her head. "A woman has a right to her body. Period."

Joey raised his hand. "Hey, hey, what about the man's rights?"

"The man's rights end at my body." Lynn pointed at her chest.

Joey huffed. "Well, that's not fair. The man's the father. He has rights too."

Lynn's breathing increased.

Here comes another argument.

"Not to my body, Joey. Don't you forget that."

"I can't believe you'd actually kill a baby without thinking about the father," Joey said as he stopped the truck in front of the Co-op.

Katie plucked *The Handmaid's Tale* from her bag and pretended to read, the best decision at the moment.

"I'll be right back." Joey slammed the door and walked into the Co-op.

Lynn followed him with her eyes, brow furrowed. "What do you think?"

Let it go, Lynn.

Katie fingered the pages. "I don't know."

Lynn smacked the outside of the truck door through the open window. The bang shook Katie. "How could you not know? Hasn't that novel taught you anything?"

"This isn't Gilead."

"Yeah, well, it could be, if we don't always keep up the fight for our rights."

Lynn wore an expression unfamiliar to Katie. The determination in her chin, yes, Katie recognized that from running. But there was something else she'd never seen before. It almost looked like hatred.

Though the air conditioning was off, Katie shivered.

#

Katie stopped herself before rounding the hall corner, alerted by rising voices.

"I don't care about that." Lynn sounded as if she was about to cry.

"But I do," Joey said. "It's the chance of a lifetime.

Getting into the UT Business School is all I ever wanted."

"We agreed you'd go to Memphis." Lynn sniffed. "Besides, you just want to go there because she's going there."

Who?

"You think this is about Katie?"

Her heart raced.

"It's pretty obvious how you feel about her."

"If it's so obvious why don't you tell me." A locker door slammed. Before she could move, Joey rounded the corner, bumped into her, and knocked her books to the ground.

"Sorry." He picked up her books and shoved them at her. "Here." He continued his departure with an apparent intensity to go anywhere but back.

Katie rounded the corner as Lynn stifled a cry. She put a hand on Lynn's shoulder, but Lynn shrugged it off and wouldn't look at her.

"I'm okay."

"What happened?" Katie dialed in the three-digit code on the Master Lock and opened the orange metal locker door.

Lynn sniffed again. "Wouldn't you like to know."

I'd like to know how Joey feels about me.

She wiped her dampening palm on the back of her jeans. "What do you mean by that?"

44

"Do you like Joey?"

Katie forced a half-smile. "Of course. We've been best friends since middle school."

Lynn's eyes narrowed. "You ever kiss him?"

Katie glanced at her phone. She was late for warmup.

"No. I really gotta——"

Lynn swung her backpack over her shoulder. "He's a great kisser." She flashed Katie a coy smile. "I taught him everything he knows."

I didn't need to hear that.

"That's nice." Katie closed the locker door and leaned against it, a sliver of light from the skylight catching her eye. The droplets on the outside of the hallway skylight from the early spring shower glistened in the sunlight.

Lynn slammed her locker door. "I'm so done with high school. Guys are too much trouble. It must be all the testosterone in their bodies." She glanced at Katie's bare legs. "Come on, let's go grab an ice cream."

Katie avoided eye contact. "You know I'm going to track practice."

"Yeah, that's right, I forgot. Gotta stay fit and firm for all the guys. Tease."

Katie followed Lynn toward the exit. "Hey, that's not fair. How many guys do you see me dating?"

They reached the school metal-framed glass doors. "You want them to want you. That's why you run."

"I run because that's the only way I can get out of this place. I need that scholarship."

Lynn tossed her green canvas backpack on the brick wall. "Yeah, that's right. The scholarship I didn't get."

"That's not my fault."

Lynn eyed Katie, then slowly smiled. "Okay, then."

Katie's tension eased. "Why don't you come back for one final fling?"

"After seven years, I hate running."

"But you used to love it."

"That was then, this is now. They don't have track at Southwest Tennessee Community College." Lynn seemed to draw out the full name of the school with intentionality and coldness.

Katie felt the uncomfortable rift between them creep back in. A whistle at the track blew. "I gotta go."

Lynn grabbed Katie's shirttail and spun her around to face her. "You never answered my question."

I thought we were done talking about Joey. Katie felt her face fluster. "I told you, we're just friends."

Lynn cocked her head. "Not that."

Lynn could shift gears in a conversation faster than an Indy race driver. "Then what?"

"What I asked yesterday. Where do you stand on abortion?"

The coach was going to make her run an extra lap for every minute she was late for drills, and Lynn knew that. "Do we have to talk about this now?"

"I just thought you'd be for it, given Evan."

The urgency of track practice vaporized. "What?"

"Your mom would still be here if—"

"If what?" Katie felt a fierceness in her neck and face beyond any anger she'd felt in her entire eighteen years. Yet it was tinged with the guilt of knowing Lynn wasn't completely wrong.

The silence between them was heavy. Katie realized her fists were clenched. She took a step back and nearly fell off the curb.

Lynn slid off the brick wall. "I'm sorry. I had no right to go there."

Katie breathed deep. "Mom loved Evan. She loved all of us."

"I never told you this." Lynn's voice was barely above a whisper. "I never told anyone this. My aunt, the one from Ireland, told me what really happened to my grandmother."

"I thought you said she caught pneumonia or something?" Katie shifted impatiently.

Lynn narrowed her eyes, which meant she was skeptical, or about to proclaim some deep secret, or something completely different. She would scowl when happy, sad, angry, or tired. She probably frowned in her sleep. "That's what I thought. Nope. In 1971 she was butchered. Because she couldn't get a legal abortion."

Another whistle blew, and Katie glanced at her bag. "I have to go."

Lynn grabbed Katie's arm. "Wait."

"What?"

Lynn paused, opened her mouth and drew in a short breath as if about to speak, then pressed her lips back together. "Never mind. Enjoy your run," she finally said.

#

The three friends stood tall together in their gowns and wide grins after they'd flung their caps in the air, along with the other seventy-two graduating seniors at the ceremony's conclusion.

Lynn held her phone up. "Selfie time." She took the picture and fiddled with the phone, thumbs moving at near light speed. "Epic. It's on Instagram now."

Joey put his arm around Lynn and studied the photo. "What a trio. We've come a long way."

Lynn pointed to Katie's orange University of Tennessee cap. "You nervous about Knoxville?"

"Why would I be nervous with my big adopted brother to look after me?" She hugged Joey's midsection with her right arm.

Lynn wagged a playful finger at Joey. "Well, don't look after her too closely." Any expressions of jealousy had faded since the locker incident. Katie never asked Lynn about it, and Lynn never offered to discuss it. Somewhere along the line, Joey and Lynn had made up, and Katie was fine with that.

Joey seemed lost in thought. "We'll be back every weekend."

"You, not me. Got to keep the scholarship, remember?" Katie said. She glanced at Lynn, instantly regretting bringing up the award, but Lynn did not seem perturbed.

Joey chuckled. "Right, until the social life butts in. Oh, wait, running is your social life."

"A social life is overrated," Katie said.

Lynn grabbed Joey's arm. "You just haven't met the right man. I'm glad I did."

Katie and Lynn's eyes locked, and Lynn frowned slightly. Katie broke the stare and turned to the family reunion area.

Her father waved, wearing a forced smile. What would happen to him, once she was at college and Evan was in the special care facility? He'd be alone.

She mindlessly picked at the raised letters of her name on the diploma, then slammed the holder shut. Her escape was finally at hand. Why didn't she feel better?

6

College (2015)

Katie sat next to Joey on the warm aluminum bleachers, thankful that for one weekend he did not go home to Nortonville. The lure of the number one team coming to play football had been too much for him, he had said.

She surveyed the vast interior of Neyland Stadium from their seats in the University of Tennessee student section. "I have never seen so many people in my life."

Joey wiped nacho cheese from the corner of his lip. "Crazy, isn't it?"

"I'm glad you stayed. I've always wanted to see a game here."

"Me too." His phone buzzed. "Lynn wants a shot."

He took a selfie with her, then warily smiled. "I think she's still jealous of you."

She forced a chuckle and studied her popcorn. "There's no reason for that. Besides, you drive home to see her every weekend. One away from her isn't going to kill her."

"She's not loving community college life, that's for sure."

She popped a few kernels in her mouth. "It's only been a bit more than a month."

A student behind her slurred a derogatory statement about Alabama. Katie leaned closer. "I didn't realize how many drunk people were at these things."

Joey chuckled. "Yup. I hear some never even make it into the game. Just tailgate."

The majority of the fans erupted in a cheer after the Tennessee safety intercepted an Alabama pass. Katie high-fived Joey as a splash of beer landed on her shoulder.

She turned and glared at the guy behind her. "Hey. Thanks a lot."

The student gave her a sloppy grin. "Sorry about that, hon. Wanna let me make it up to you?" He put his right hand on her waist and leaned in.

The sharp smell of alcohol made her stomach

turn. She was leaning away when Joey pushed the student roughly back in his seat.

Joey pointed at him. "Learn some manners."

The student rose unsteadily. "How 'bout you teach me, redneck?"

Joey stood fully erect, eye-to-eye with the student standing on the row above them. He pushed up the brim of his denim cap with the orange T, his jaw clenched. "You really don't want to go there."

Katie knew that face. Joey was mad.

The drunk student snorted, shrugged to his buddy, then sat down.

Tension eased from Katie's chest and a warm queasiness formed in her stomach. No one had ever defended her like that.

Stop. He's Lynn's.

Joey maintained his stance for a moment before he turned and lowered himself into his seat. The sternness of his features faded. He handed her a couple of napkins. "Here. You need these more than I do."

She blotted the beer spills on her orange Vols T-shirt. "Thanks, but I've seen you eat."

He laughed. "True, true."

He resumed his attack on the nachos, offering her some, but the borderline nausea still hadn't lifted.

When he glanced back at her, she realized she'd

been staring. She had never seen this side of Joey——strong and protective.

"What?" he said. "Do I have cheese on my chin again?"

"Yeah." Though he didn't.

She turned back to the game. His chivalry wasn't a glimpse of deep inner love. That was Joey being Joey. And Joey was Lynn's.

At least for part of a weekend, though, she didn't feel so lonely.

#

"Good to be home." Katie smiled as Joey parked the old faded-red Chevy truck in front of her house.

Joey flashed a lopsided grin. "You didn't have to wait for fall break. You could have come home any of the weekends I did."

"You know I couldn't. I may have been a star runner here, but there I'm just one of many. I can't lose my scholarship. Every practice, every opportunity——"

He held up a hand. "I know, I know. Gotta put in those miles. I get it. I still run too, remember?"

"Yeah, but your college career doesn't depend on it."

Joey rested a casual arm on the back of Katie's seat.

Almost as if——but no. "I'll call you when we're ready to go out later. Lynn's looking forward to it."

Third wheel again.

The open barn door beckoned. "I may not be able to come. It depends on how Evan is."

"Any news?"

Katie's eye went to the empty swing. "Dad wouldn't say. He sounded funny on the phone last night though."

Joey tapped the steering wheel with his graduation ring. "Okay, you just let me know."

She bounded out of his truck when she spied her father in work clothes next to the Kubota tractor beside the barn.

Her father rose, lug nut wrench in hand, and wiped his hands with the ever-present red bandanna. "Give me a hug."

"How's Evan?"

Her father avoided eye contact and repeatedly wiped the same spot of the tool. "He's fine. The home said he just had an event." He stopped the polishing and looked at Katie. "He misses you."

"I miss him. I thought he was doing well there."

"He is. Just separation anxiety." He stuffed the rag in his overalls pocket and kneeled next to the rear wheel of the tractor with the wrench.

"What's up with the tractor?" she asked.

He scratched his head. "Back wheel is losing air. I'm not sure from where. I'm going to take it off and dump it in the old aluminum trough to find the leak. Want to help?"

"Sure. You know I love helping you."

He gave her a sly grin. "C'mon, now. You've been wanting to get away from the farm since you were twelve."

"Well, maybe I don't know what I really want." The stack of hay bales in the barn hallway caught her attention. "Why's that down here?"

"Your old man forgot to get the last load of hay in September. Glad Mr. Burns still had alfalfa available."

He must have been distracted by everything that had happened with Evan. He wouldn't meet her eye again.

"Dad, you did the right thing putting him in that place. It's a first-class facility. You couldn't handle it on your own."

He wiped his brow again. His sweat seemed excessive for a crisp fall day. "I guess."

She walked over to the hay stack and leaned in to savor the sweet aroma of the grass. "Want me to put it up before I go see Evan?"

He arched his spine. "That would be great. My back's acting up again."

She hauled the square bails up to the loft. There was enough hay up there now to last the winter for their three horses. When she finished, she brushed off her jeans. The flattened tire remained on the ground beside her father. He should have at least gotten it into the trough by now. "Is it fixable?"

"Dunno. I'm gonna take the other off since I've got the trough filled. And I'm going to need your help getting them in." He rubbed the small of his back.

"You need to hire a helper."

He removed the wrench from one nut and moved diagonally to the next. "I have one now. For a few days anyway. Are you planning to spend time with your friends?"

She put her hands in her jeans front pockets. "I think Joey and Lynn want their alone time."

He grunted as he pushed on the handle of the wrench. "How're they doing? I haven't seen them since y'all left for school."

Katie walked around the backside of the tractor. "Oh, I guess they're fine. She's not dealing well with community college though. And with him away."

He paused to wipe his sweaty brow again. "Separation is hard on anyone, especially young folks. They say absence makes the heart grow fonder, but sometimes I don't believe it."

She propped her arm against the roll bar. "Why's that, Dad?"

He broke the torque on the nut and moved on to the next, pausing to rub his knuckles. "Well, when you're young, time is magical. It's not like when you get older and it becomes rarer to find something new. But being a young adult, everything is new. New people, new distractions, new situations, new understandings about the world around you." He loosened the last nut. "There. Done."

She caught a glance out the main barn doors and imagined Evan happily swinging. "I miss Mom."

Her father paused his search for the hydraulic jack and put his arm around her. She leaned into him. "Your mom was an amazing woman."

She forced a glance at the horseshoe nailed above the barn entrance. *Why did I receive all the family's good luck?*

#

Katie glanced at Joey from the pages of *Go Set a Watchman.* She didn't want to provoke a confrontation, but his two-hour silent treatment on the drive back to Knoxville maddened her.

He caught her eye. "How is it?"

His words startled her. She had expected the noncommunication to continue for the rest of the trip. "What?"

"The book. How is it?"

"Seriously, you care?"

"Well, yeah. I loved *To Kill A Mockingbird*. We read it in sixth grade, remember?"

Right. We were in the same reading group together in Mrs. Allen's class. With Lynn.

"Yeah. I'm just surprised you do. You're not exactly a voracious reader."

He tapped his high school graduation ring against the steering wheel, a sure sign of nervousness. "True."

"What's bothering you?"

He continued the *tap, tap, tap* and kept his eyes on the road.

No words of Harper Lee would cut through the returned tension. She eyed a sign about a tenth of a mile ahead. "There's a Subway at the Parsons exit. Let's stop."

Joey turned off the interstate. Katie was happy to step out into the crisp October air, a break from the stifling discomfort of the drive. She surveyed the sparsely occupied restaurant. "Doesn't look busy."

"Whatever."

Mr. Happy.

They ordered their sandwiches, found a table and she bit into her chicken wrap. Too much sweet onion sauce. She chewed at a measured pace and maneuvered her tongue as discreetly as possible to dislodge a filament of chicken from between two molars. Joey kept his attention focused outside the window or around the restaurant, on anything and everything but her.

She dropped the remaining half of her chicken wrap on the tray. "Okay. Stop this. Talk to me."

He shook his head.

"Come on, Joey. It's me, remember? You can tell me anything. Did I do something?" She took a long sip of her unsweetened tea.

He laid down his sandwich, drew in a deep breath, and lowered his head. "We broke up."

Again?

She let out her breath in a measured stream. "What? No. I'm sorry. What happened?"

"I dunno. She's gotten all weird on me." He picked up the sub and took a large bite.

"Like what?" Thank goodness for her wrap. Chewing would hide any hint on her face of her elation that Joey was available.

"She says she misses me, then when I'm home for the weekend she acts like she doesn't want to be around me. Wasn't like that the first couple times I came home."

"Maybe she's adjusting to the new life."

"Yeah." He stuffed the last bit into his mouth, more than an average bite size, and wiped his hands together. "We've got to get going. There's not much more to say. She said she wants her space. So I gave it to her." He raised his arms. "Fine with me. She has hers, I have mine."

She pushed away the instant hope. Joey never looked at other women during the separations, and he always returned to Lynn.

#

Each light electronic click produced by Joey's thumbs on his phone's keyboard interfered with Katie's T-chart calculations. "Do you mind? I'm trying to study. This is a library, you know."

Joey's finger dancing stopped. "Why are you even taking economics? Do you really need that to be an English teacher?"

"It's an elective."

"You could have chosen an easier one. Like nuclear physics." He returned to fiddling with his phone, paused, then turned it screen down.

She peered at him over the pages of her economics

textbook. Tight jaw. Distant gaze. It was that same look as the trip home three weeks ago.

"She did it again, didn't she?"

He rubbed his chin. "Yup. And I'm the fool."

She lowered the textbook, leaned back in her chair, and reached behind to close the door to the small study room. This time, suppressing the hope proved quite easy. "That was quick. You just made up last weekend. What's her reason this time?"

"Same old stuff. I'm too far away, I don't have a clue in life, I'm basically a loser——"

"Joey, you are not a loser."

He produced a worn tennis ball from his backpack and tossed it in one hand. "And here I was planning our Thanksgiving back home."

"She's the one with a problem. She only wants you when she can't have you. Then once she sucks you back in, the thrill is over."

"Maybe."

"Trust me. She's not right for you."

Joey's eyes brightened. He paused the solitary game of catch. "Lots of fish in the sea, right?"

One fish in particular.

Hope rose. "There's a positive attitude."

"Carla McKenzie's been sitting with me in marketing."

What?

"Maybe I'll ask her out." Joey tossed the ball into the trash can near the door behind Katie. "Barbetti, three points. Grizzlies win. What?"

She shook her head, hope dashed. "Nothing."

Carla McKenzie?

#

The crispness of the December morning air fueled a final competitive sprint. She beat him, as usual.

Joey pulled up beside her. "I can't believe how fast you are."

She smiled. "A long way from that first run to Finny."

He returned a somewhat forced smile.

She bent over to catch her breath from the morning three-mile run, but kept her eyes on him. "What is it?"

He stretched an arm above his head. "What do you mean?"

"Pissed you lost our bet? It's just a taco."

His posture loosened for a moment, then stiffened, as if he was drawing on secret energy reserves to bolster his conviction. "No. Lynn and I decided to try again."

"What? You're kidding. What about Carla?"

Joey seemed to forget who Carla was for a

moment. "Three dates. She doesn't even like football."

"Neither does Lynn, remember?"

He flipped his hair away from his face. "It's just that we've been together for so long."

The disappointment boiled from her diaphragm to her lips. Maybe she wasn't right for Joey, but Lynn definitely was wrong. "This is the worst thing you can do. She'll dump you again once it's no longer a challenge to keep you."

"Maybe."

"How many times has she made empty promises?" She caught her voice rising. "You have too much going for you to take that from her anymore."

"Whatever."

"Wake up, Joey." She stood inches from his face. "It's a game to her. Can't you see that? It's killing you. She's my best friend, but the way she's strung you along——"

"She hasn't——"

"Yes, she has. She cares more about herself than you. You don't need her to make you happy."

He looked away. "I thought you'd be happy for us," he said, voice cracking.

Her rush of adrenaline subsided. "Joey, I want you to be happy. Besides getting out of Nortonville, that's all I ever wanted." She reached out and gently placed a hand on his shoulder, still warm from the run.

"No. You're right." He cocked his head and studied her, as if suddenly realizing something. "That's funny."

"What?"

He flashed a hint of the disarming crooked smile. "You look, well, different."

She stared behind him at a crane by the river. "How so?"

"I don't know."

She continued to focus on anything but him. "You're just upset that you always lose to me." She trembled.

That was a stupid thing to say.

He kept his gaze on her, well within her personal space. She wondered if he would step back, but he didn't.

"I do want to be happy." He reached out, touched her chin, and gently directed her head upward.

The early morning sunlight caught his green irises. The rush flowed from the center of her body to her fingers and toes. Wordless, they leaned in. His lips brushed against hers, until passion buried the uncertainty.

She released the embrace. "Wow."

"Yeah. Wow."

She imagined Lynn's reaction at the news. "This is going to be complicated."

The story continues in *Fatherhood*, a full-length novel about abortion from the father's point of view, coming soon.